HOW THE HARE TOLD THE TRUTH ABOUT HIS HORSE

by Barbara K. Walker

with illustrations by Charles Mikolaycak

" HOW THE HARE TOLD THE TRUTH ABOUT HIS .. HORSE

Parents' Magazine Press / New York

Designed by Charles Mikolaycak.

For Lilian Moore

Once long ago
a man and a lion were good friends, just like brothers.

Day after day, the lion came to visit the man. Every day the lion said, "Some day, when we are truly best friends, I want you to come to visit me."

Now, the hare had watched the man and the lion. He, too, wanted to be the man's friend. What could he do to make the man want him as his friend, perhaps even as his brother?

"I know!" he said one day. "I must prove that
I am the master of the lion. But that is not easily done."

He thought and thought again. Finally he smiled. He had a good plan. Now he must try it.

He went to the man. "I would like to have you as my brother," he said. The man laughed. "Thank you, but I already have a brother. The lion is my brother."

"The lion?" The hare laughed. "The lion is nobody. Didn't you know? The lion is no more than my horse."

"Your horse?" said the man. "I cannot believe that."

The hare went home. That after-
noon, the lion came to see the man. Suddenly the man
began to laugh. "So you are the hare's horse!" he said.
"Who told
you I was the hare's horse?" asked the lion, surprised.
"The hare
himself told me," said the man. "I cannot believe it. All the
same, it may be true. After all, the hare said it was true."
The lion lashed his tail in anger. "I shall
find the hare and teach him to speak the truth," he said.

He looked here and there and everywhere.

At last he found the hare. "So you told the man I was your horse!" he said crossly. "It is a lie. You know I am not your horse."

"Of course you are not my horse," said the hare, laughing at such a foolish idea. "The man misunderstood. If I did not feel so ill, I would go and tell him myself. But, alas, I am not well enough to walk."

"Very well," said the lion, "I will carry you there. Then you can tell the man the truth."

The lion crouched
down. Carefully the hare climbed onto his back.
"Are you ready?" asked the lion.
"I am ready," said the hare.
The lion began to walk toward the man's village.
The hare swayed from side to side as the lion walked.

"Wait!" called the hare. "I am becoming very dizzy. I cannot go to tell the man after all."
The lion stopped.
"You MUST tell the man," he said. "He will not be my brother if he thinks I am no better than the hare's horse. What can I do to make you ride more comfortably?"

The hare thought for a minute. "Perhaps we could make a bridle from that grapevine over there," he said. "We could put the bridle in your mouth, and that would give me something to hold on to."

"All right," said the lion, and they made a fine bridle from the grapevine. It was passed through the lion's mouth. The lion crouched down again. Once more, the hare climbed on his back. The lion began walking again toward the man's village.

Slap! Slap! The hare began slapping at the flies around him. "Wait!" he called. "I cannot go to tell the man after all. These flies are making me very dizzy."

The lion stopped. "You MUST tell the man," he said. "I do not wish to have him believe such an untruth. What can we do to drive away the flies?"

"If I had a small whip to hold," said the hare, "I believe I could drive them away. See. There is a bush by the path. We could take a small branch from that."

The lion broke off a small branch as a whip. Carefully the hare trimmed off all the leaves. "Now!" he said. "That should do. Now I can manage nicely, I think."

The lion crouched down. Once more, the hare climbed on his back. He held the ends of the bridle in one front paw and the whip in the other. Carefully the lion began to walk. Tug-tug went the bridle. Slap-slap went the whip. Yes, the hare managed very nicely.

At last they came to the man's house. He was sitting outside. When he saw them coming, he began to laugh.

"You will not laugh when you hear the truth spoken by the hare," said the lion with great dignity. "Tell him, hare."

"O man," said the hare, sitting proudly on the back of the lion, "you can see for yourself whether or not the lion is my horse. The judgment of your eyes is more sound than anything either I or the lion could say."

Too late, the lion recognized the truth: that he had indeed become the hare's horse. As for the hare, he was well satisfied. And the man? He has laughed each time the story has been told down the long years till now.

Barbara K. Walker has six books on the Parents' Magazine Press list, including HOW THE HARE TOLD THE TRUTH ABOUT HIS HORSE; THE ROUND SULTAN AND THE STRAIGHT ANSWER; THE MOUSE AND THE ELEPHANT; STARGAZER TO THE SULTAN; WATERMELONS, WALNUTS AND THE WISDOM OF ALLAH; and THE DANCING PALM TREE AND OTHER NIGERIAN FOLKTALES; and she has contributed countless stories and poems to HUMPTY DUMPTY'S MAGAZINE.

Her husband, Dr. Warren S. Walker, also an author of many books, is a professor at Texas Tech University. The Walkers live in Lubbock, Texas.

Charles Mikolaycak is the illustrator of GREAT WOLF AND THE GOOD WOODSMAN, published by Parents' Magazine Press and selected as one of the Fifty Best Books of the Year by the American Institute of Graphic Arts in 1967. More recently he has illustrated THE GORGAN'S HEAD, and has written and illustrated THE BOY WHO TRIED TO CHEAT DEATH. He has received a gold medal for art direction and numerous citations from the Society of Illustrators. Mr. Mikolaycak and his wife live in New York City.